THE

CHRISTMAS

A Romantic Fairy Tale

Jean C. Joachim

Moonlight Books

Best wishes!
Jean Joachim

A Moonlight Books Novel
Sweet Romantic Fairy Tale
The House-Sitter's Christmas
Holiday Hearts series

Copyright © 2017 Jean C. Joachim
Cover design by Jean Joachim
Edited by Sherri Good
Proofread by Renee Waring
All cover art and logo copyright © 2017 by Moonlight Books

PUBLISHER
Moonlight Books

Dedication

To all who love holidays, happy endings, and believe in fairy tales.

Special Dedication

To the late Marilyn Reisse Lee,
my dearest friend.
And
Homer, my muse

Acknowledgment
Thank you for your support:
My readers. Without you there would be no books.
And to Steve Dimitriou, for his insightful suggestions
regarding my cover.

A Word from the Author

THE HOUSE-SITTER'S Christmas is a romantic, holiday fairy tale. It was written originally as a romantic serial, with an episode released each day during the month of December. It's not a chaptered novella or short story but consists of short episodes instead. There is an element of suspense woven into the fabric of this tale, as well.

Although the story could continue, there is a happy ending. But those who know me, recognize that characters may stay with me, reappearing in additional books or short stories, sometimes a year or more later. I don't swear that this is the final chapter for Laura and C.W.

However, the ending wraps up the events in this novella. If you wish to have another story with these folks, please tell me. You can contact me by email (jean@nowandforeverbooks.com) or on Facebook and make your wishes known.

I hope you enjoy this story. Thank you for reading my work.

Jean C. Joachim

P.S. Look for George's story next year.

Episode One

LAURA FLEMING'S PULSE kicked up as the bus approached the Lincoln Tunnel. Something magical happened whenever she crossed over from upstate onto Manhattan Island. And, it being a week before Christmas only made it more fantastic.

The Port Authority Bus Terminal was as bloated with people as usual. Mr. C. W. Banley had arranged for a car to pick her up. She was the hired help—the house-sitter, paid to keep his majestic townhouse occupied and to care for his cat while he traveled on business over the holidays.

This was Laura's third year house-sitting for C.W., as she affectionately referred to him—but never to his face. In fact, she'd never met him. What mattered was her chance to step into the ultimate Christmas fantasy, occupying a grand townhouse on West 81st Street for three delicious weeks.

A man in a livery outfit stood on the crowded sidewalk, holding a sign that read *Laura Fleming*. She approached him, vouched for her identity, and slid into the comfortable vehicle. He closed the door, and they were off, wending their way through the dense, holiday traffic.

"First time in the City?" he asked, while they waited at a stop light.

"Oh, no. I've been coming during the holidays for several years."

"It's a beautiful, if crowded, time to be here."

"I love it. I live in the country. During the winter, I get cabin fever with all the snow and ice."

"You own a place here too?"

She laughed, her light brown hair swinging with the motion. "Oh, no. I could never afford that. I'm the house-sitter."

"Now that's a great gig!"

"You bet it is," she agreed.

Laura looked out the window as the chauffeur maneuvered his way through congested Amsterdam Avenue. All the restaurants, and even the delis, had strings of Christmas lights. She raised her gaze to the apartment buildings and spied many with holiday decorations or elaborately decorated trees in the windows.

He pulled up to the gorgeous, Neo-Renaissance townhouse. The driver set her small suitcase on the sidewalk. He refused a tip, saying he'd already been paid, then handed her a sealed envelope. Laura gazed at the beautiful, cream-colored building with windows lined in black. A large, circular, black, wrought iron staircase beckoned her.

The winter sky turned teal blue as the sun set. She climbed the steps to the carved, wooden door. A wreath of evergreens, red berries, and pine cones hung there, welcoming her. The sharp wind penetrated her coat, making her shiver. She ripped open the envelope and retrieved the front door key. She smiled. Mr. Banley was a bear about security and would never leave a key under a mat. Eager to get to the antique pot of hot chocolate Maeve, the housekeeper, always left for her on the little wooden table by the fireplace in the study, Laura wondered if there would be a chocolate croissant, or a scone, waiting too. She licked her lips as she crossed the threshold into luxury she could only dream about.

Episode Two

LAURA CLIMBED THE STAIRS to a small room facing the street. Though only big enough for a leather loveseat, wing chair, and small round table, Mr. Banley had managed to find space for a little tree in the corner. A small tub of ornaments and lights sat parked neatly under the table.

C.W. Banley had left New York early in December and delighted in returning to a home decorated for the holiday.

There were two more trees, a large one in the living room and a small one in her bedroom, each with its own set of decorations. An extra tub of ornaments and lights resided next to a box of candles and another envelope. As usual, he expected her to decorate them all.

Laura loved the task, having the freedom to place exquisite pieces wherever she wanted. After heating the flue, to create a draft, and lighting the fire, she eased back in the seat, and opened the envelope with her instructions. As she read, she sipped on the finest chocolate to warm her bones and nibbled on a scone.

While thinking about which room to tackle first, her gaze rested on a photograph of C.W. and his nephew. The white-haired gentleman was handsome, though distinguished might better describe his looks. The strong family resemblance in his nephew struck her. Two good-looking men. She wondered if she'd ever meet C.W. and guessed probably not.

Opening her phone, she played holiday music, starting with *Carol of the Bells*. She surveyed the tree and opened the tub, then fished out the strings of lights. Humming along with Nat King Cole, she listened for the crackle of the logs and breathed in the strong, fresh scent of pine.

This was a traditional Christmas, her traditional Christmas, even if she celebrated it alone. Actually, not quite alone. Jasper, a male, orange tabby cat, scampered into the room. He rubbed against her legs, in greeting, then hopped up on the loveseat and curled up to watch her work.

Episode Three

RITZ HOTEL, 15 PLACE Vendôme, Paris, 4 a.m.

Craig Watson Banley, phone in hand, perched on a sofa in his hotel suite, sipping excellent hot chocolate and staring out the window. He couldn't sleep.

"I suppose I should check to make sure my house-sitter arrived. How do I access that security crap, George?"

Bathrobe sashed, George Manfred, Craig's indispensable assistant and father substitute, joined his boss. C.W. didn't feel uncomfortable rousing his aide at such an ungodly hour because part of his job was to keep C.W. company, even at odd hours.

"It's supposed to be on your phone. Let me see. I think we have to add the app." George divested the thirty-five-year-old of his cell and fiddled with it like a master. Craig chuckled.

"People in the office would laugh if they could see that you're more proficient with that fucking thing than I am."

George grinned but continued to work his magic. "There! We have the Safehouse Security app installed. Now, let's see. We have to find your house. We need a password. Want to use the usual?"

"*Jasper*? Yeah, sure." Craig pushed to his feet and strolled to the window. Paris in December was a charming place. But then, Paris in any season was breathtaking. He wondered what it would be like to be here with a beautiful woman instead of old

George. He sighed. Not happening this year, maybe not next either. In fact, there was no special one in the foreseeable future.

Maybe if his dotty old uncle decided to stop playing house in the mountains of Colorado with young women, Craig could have a life. Uncle Chet, Chester William Banley, had had enough of business. Now, sex, eating, and drinking were his major pastimes. Craig wished he had stock in the company that made Viagra.

When Uncle Chet stepped off the business merry-go-round, he'd handed the reins of his multinational businesses over to his favorite nephew—in fact, his only nephew, Craig. The old bachelor had kept the family fortunes alive for forty years. Now, he'd decided to have the life he'd missed. How could Craig blame him?

"Got it! Here you go," George said. Craig joined him and listened while the older man explained how to access the new security system installed in his New York City townhouse. A broken window and a theft had convinced the young billionaire to install protection, including placing tiny cameras everywhere.

Craig sat back and fiddled with his cell. "Let's see. Hmm. It should show me someplace if anyone's been through the front door. Hold it! Whoa! Yeah. I see." A fuzzy picture of a person from the top showed on the screen. He frowned. "I guess that's Laura Fleming."

"Did you tell Miss Fleming about the cameras?"

"Nope. Security doesn't work if everyone knows about it."

"You expect her to steal from you? She's been minding the house for three years now. And nothing's gone missing, has it?"

"No, but you can't be too careful. These old biddies with no life. Who knows what they'll do?"

"If you felt that way, why'd you hire her again?"

Craig shrugged. "Guess it's the cookies and stuff she leaves behind."

"You mean, the only Christmas present you get from someone who doesn't have to give you one?"

"George."

"That was unkind. Still. I don't think you're being quite fair."

"Success isn't built on fair."

"I suppose not. I've got email to check. See you later," George said, heading for his room.

Craig knit his brows. George's disapproval stung. The young man took another sip of chocolate, then scrolled through the boring film of his house. As night came, unoccupied rooms appeared black. He was just about to shut it off when a room with brilliant illumination popped up. It was Miss Fleming's bedroom.

He loved that room, all white, and clean—elegant, actually. The camera picked up the fire in the fireplace, the bed—there were wrapped presents there—and the tree. She had already decorated. As always, it was exquisite. For an old lady, she had damn good taste.

Then, there was movement. *Holy Hell*! A woman appeared on the screen, and she was taking off her clothes. Getting ready for bed, he assumed. Geez! A flush of embarrassment heated his face. He should turn that off right away. But he couldn't. Long, dark hair dipped below her shoulders as delicate hands lifted her sweater. It was like a slow, private striptease.

Blood pumped to his groin. *Shut it off. Shut it off!* George would kill him, but he was glued to the erotic scene unfolding in front of his eyes. She unzipped her pants and stepped out of them. Only wearing a lacy red bra and matching panties, she stopped to fold her other garments.

If that was Laura Fleming, she was no old biddy! He prayed she'd come back into view. As if she'd heard him, she returned with a nightgown in one hand. She easily unhooked her bra and stepped out of the panties. Craig could hardly breathe. Even the twitching between his legs couldn't distract him completely.

She stretched and did a few bending exercises before slipping the gown over her head. The woman had a body to die for. She'd been coming to his house for three years, and he'd had no idea. George should get a bonus for suggesting he install the security system.

Episode Four

LAURA PADDED DOWNSTAIRS in her flimsy nightgown and silk robe. The house was warm enough so that she didn't need the flannel she wore at home. Jasper was right behind her.

She opened a can of food for him and put on coffee. Last year, it had taken three days to figure out Mr. Banley's fancy coffeemaker. Soon, the delicious aroma of the fresh brew wafted through the air.

She fried up two eggs and toasted two pieces of whole wheat bread. Maeve always made sure there was breakfast fare in the fridge and a container of her famous stew in the freezer. Sitting at the kitchen table in the company of Jasper, who sat cleaning himself after his meal, she gazed out the window. Many of the townhouses on 82nd Street had decorations in the back. A few Christmas trees were visible through glass doors and big windows.

The kitchen was spacious, for New York City, and well-equipped. She wondered why. She'd read about Mr. Banley, an older bachelor. Why would he have every modern convenience in his kitchen? Maybe because he wanted all the luxury money could buy? He was certainly rich enough. She shrugged. So much the better for her. Using a top-of-the-line food processor for her cookie dough made life easier.

She made a list of places to visit. Of course, the tree in Rockefeller Center and the windows at Lord & Taylor, plus a stroll down Fifth Avenue, if it wasn't too cold. Then, there were the Christmas trees in the Natural History Museum and the Metropolitan Museum. Mr. Banley had left his membership cards on the bureau in her room.

Tonight, dinner at McGinty's Bar & Grill on Amsterdam. She needed to call a few friends she'd made on her forays into New York to house-sit. When she finished eating, she cleaned up and hit the shower. Dressed in fleece pants and a down jacket, she read the instructions for the security system one more time before locking up. She memorized the code straight away.

Of course, with a home as grand as this, loaded with priceless antiques and original artwork, Mr. Banley needed security. She wondered why he hadn't thought of it before. Having the alarm on the front door made sense and, being alone, she enjoyed the new feeling of safety.

As she walked to the bus across the street, she wondered if Sean, the bartender at McGinty's, would remember her from last year. She hoped he did. With his smiling blue eyes, ready wit, and dark hair he was a handsome addition to the friendly eatery.

Of course, she couldn't bring him home or anything like that. Not that she'd planned to sleep with him. She hardly knew him. But if things did heat up while she was there, she'd have to go to his place. No guests or strangers of any kind were to be allowed in the house. That was rule number one. She'd not break it, out of respect. But if she did, who would know?

Episode Five

CRAIG HAD NOT CHECKED on Laura again. He and George put their heads together to prepare for their meetings in Turkey, Italy, Marseille, and Sweden. After his wife had died, and his children had scattered, George had said he hadn't minded missing Christmas. Craig offered the man a generous bonus for traveling with him.

He hadn't forgotten about the security system and the luscious Miss Fleming. He'd made sure to be too busy, and then too tired, to spy on her again. Guilt and curiosity nagged at him. He needed to see her again, but dressed, of course.

What was a pretty girl like her doing spending the holidays alone in New York City? Why wasn't she married with kids? Of course, it was none of his business. He needed to stay focused on setting up deals for the coming year and not get distracted by some mysterious woman living in his home. Easier said than done.

On their last day in Paris, Craig and George dined in their suite.

"I just want to check and make sure the house is okay."

"I'm sure Miss Fleming would notify Maeve if there was a problem," George said.

"Humor me." Craig touched the app on his cell with a shaky finger. The first room up was the living room. He gasped. Miss

Fleming had gone above and beyond. The tree was splendid. Red and white lights twinkled, highlighting gold and white balls. Special ornaments, randomly placed, drew the eye up and down.

"It's beautiful," he muttered.

"What? Her?"

"No. The tree."

"Oh. Have you seen her?" George threw out the question casually, focusing his attention on his food.

Caught off guard, Craig flushed, heat rocketing to his face. Tongue-tied, he stared at his wine glass.

The silence drew George's attention. "What? Cat got your tongue?"

Still unable to face his companion, Craig glanced out the window.

"Oh no. Oh my God! You have seen her, haven't you?"

Craig nodded, still looking away. "Yes. All of her."

George bolted out of his chair. "What? What are you saying?"

"I didn't mean to do it. I didn't know she was getting ready for bed," Craig pleaded.

"You mean you watched her disrobe?"

Craig nodded.

"Oh, lordy. That's a crime, isn't it?"

"Not if it's your own home, I don't think. I didn't mean to. It just happened."

"How many times have you watched her undress?" George cocked an eyebrow

"Once! Just once! I swear."

"A likely story." The older man picked up his wine glass.

"Honest, George. I wouldn't lie to you. I will admit I've wanted to, but I haven't. I mean that's too low."

"Yes, even for you."

"What do you mean?"

"Ah, it's the frat boy in you."

"Here she comes. She's dressed. You can look," Craig said.

"How old is she?"

"Maybe thirty? Hard to tell. The picture's grainy."

"Damn. Too young for me." George frowned.

"Damn right. But perfect for me. Except she's there, and I'm here."

The two men watched Laura place swag over the mantle. The fire burned beneath. She fanned herself with her hand, then reached for the hem of her sweater.

"Craig! Shut it off!"

But Laura pulled the sweater over her head quickly. Craig let out a breath when he saw she had a T-shirt on underneath.

"Oh, thank God," George said.

"Scared you, huh?" Craig snickered.

George took a healthy drink and sat back. "You can shut that off now."

"I wonder what she sounds like."

"Call her, why don't you?"

"I don't have her phone number."

"Call her on your landline."

"She'll never pick up."

"Chicken?" George cocked an eyebrow.

Of course he was, but he'd never admit it. Besides, what would he say? Gee, you look great naked on camera? Or how about, I thought you were an old hag and am shocked to find out you're young and pretty? Uh, no.

"What could I say? And if I did call and scare her off, then the house'll be vacant, and Jasper'll starve."

"Oh, right, right. Good excuse. Quick thinking. I know you're afraid. It's okay. I would be too." George laughed and drained his glass.

Episode Six

LAURA SMOOTHED OUT a piece of paper she'd brought from home. It was the list of everything happening during her time in NYC. At least the stuff on the Upper West Side. Tonight, there'd be carolers. Saturday was the Christmas sing-along at the West Side Presbyterian Church.

This morning, she'd be meeting Sean McGinty for breakfast. He'd be at the bar but promised to take her somewhere nice.

She'd showered and dressed in a red velour dress. One glance in the mirror, and she'd swear she was pregnant. It was the cut of the garment, the Empire waist. She shook her head, that was the style, and they weren't selling much else. She zipped up knee-high black suede boots.

A red print, chiffon scarf slung around her neck hid a bit of cleavage. Women like her, with slightly larger breasts, often showed more than they wanted to with today's necklines. She applied light makeup, fluffed her hair one more time, and ventured out into the crisp morning air.

The sun was hiding behind gray clouds. Bright lights on Columbus Avenue set a festive mood and she found herself humming *Jingle Bell Rock* as she strolled down the street. The bar was closed, but she saw Sean inside, setting up. He came to the door, took her hand, and kissed her palm, making her giggle.

"You're lookin' lovelier than ever, Miss Laura."

"Thank you, Sean. Where are we going?"

"A little place on 83rd." He shrugged on a jacket and laced his fingers with hers.

The pretty pink sign of *Le Salon du Monde* swayed slightly in the brisk breeze. They descended four steps into the cozy eatery. At eight in the morning, they were the only patrons.

A man, with menus tucked under his arm, sat them away from the door. Pretty, square tables, covered with decorative ceramic tile in flower patterns, dotted the little space.

"Chocolat or Café?" the waiter asked.

"Oh, chocolat, *s'il vous plaît,*" Laura answered.

"Coffee for me," Sean said.

The server smiled and left.

Feeling reckless, Laura ordered a chocolate chip waffle with raspberry butter.

"Where the hell is the bacon and eggs?" Sean asked, turning the menu from front to back.

"I think a bacon omelet is the closest you'll get," she pointed out.

"Pretty snobby here, aren't they?"

"I think it's charming."

"And romantic?" he asked, wiggling his eyebrows.

Laura felt color suffuse her cheeks. Obviously, Sean had more than breakfast on his mind. But how did she feel? Did she come to C.W. Banley's house to have an affair with Sean?

He took her hand.

"How've you been?"

"Fine. Looking forward to Christmas in the City."

"I've been thinking about you. Haven't met anyone as pretty, or as chatty, as you."

"Do I talk too much?" Her hand flew to her mouth.

"Not at all. Don't misunderstand. I like what you have to say. You don't talk about stupid celebrities and crap like that."

"Thanks." She cast her gaze to the tabletop. Sean was turning up the heat. Well, was she going to get intimate with him? And if so, where? Certainly not in C.W. Banley's bed. A giggle escaped her throat at the thought of what the old gentleman would think if he knew.

"Did I cross your mind at all? Maybe once or twice since last year?" Sean was now caressing the back of her hand with his thumb.

"Why do you think I came back?"

Hell, she wasn't going to decide about having a fling with Sean on an empty stomach, that was for sure. She sat back and gazed at the twinkle in his eye. As he was about to speak, the food arrived. Soon, she'd be full with no excuse left to avoid his intentions.

Episode Seven

AFTER BREAKFAST, SEAN insisted on walking Laura home.

"It's not dangerous at ten o'clock in the morning."

"So?" He took her hand.

"Don't you have work to do? Setting up for lunch?"

"My sister, Maureen, said she'd take over. I have time."

Laura swallowed. What was she going to do? She wasn't supposed to let anyone in the house, and that included Sean. But he'd expect to come in, and maybe he'd expect more. Still, it would be their secret. She pulled her bottom lip between her teeth. Would it be only a few minutes?

They passed a small bookstore with lights strung around the window. And a Starbucks.

"I love it here. Like a small town in the big city," Sean mused.

"If you want to see a small town, you should come to Pine Grove, sometime," she said.

He quirked an eyebrow at her. "Is that an invitation?"

Sean in her house was a different matter. Would she invite him? Could he take the time away from McGinty's?

"And what would you do if I did invite you?"

A look of surprise passed over his face.

"I thought so. You're married to McGinty's. A weekend away would put you in cardiac arrest."

"No one can run that place like I can. And I do quite well, if I do say so myself."

"Glad to hear it. Then, breakfast didn't break you," she replied.

"I could take you on a World Cruise, Miss Laura Fleming, and it wouldn't break me," Sean said, stopping. "This is it, right? Old man Banley's?"

She nodded.

"What's on the first floor," he asked, peering in the shuttered window.

"Maeve told me that's where he has his office."

"Pretty convenient. Walk downstairs and you're at work. Well, are you gonna let me take a look at the place?" He put one foot on the step.

"Of course. Come on." She tripped up the metal staircase with him behind.

She unlocked the door and turned to him.

"Before I let you in, you have to promise not to tell anyone. Understood?"

"The old man's that dotty?"

"Those are the rules, and I've always obeyed them."

"Until you fell under the spell of Sean McGinty," he responded.

"Promise?"

"I swear. Cross my heart," he said, drawing an "x" over the left side of his chest.

Laura steered him through the small entryway into the living room. It was a grand room with high ceiling, crown molding, and a white marble fireplace. The room was painted a lemon-chiffon yellow with bright, white trim.

"Holy smokes! You weren't kiddin' when you said he had bucks." Sean strolled around the room, staring.

Over the mantle was a portrait of a couple. Laura guessed it was Banley's parents or grandparents, probably the first to build this place. A stiff-backed sofa, facing the fireplace, was flanked by two wing chairs. The furniture was upholstered in a blue, yellow, and white striped fabric.

A small rolltop desk hugged one corner. Two long windows sat close together. They viewed 81st Street and the museum. Gauzy white curtains filtered out the bright, southern light.

As Laura stood at the window, Sean stole up behind her. He snaked his arms around her waist and kissed her neck.

"Lovely, Laura. You belong here."

She laughed. "I wish. Nope. Just for a few weeks a year."

"Can I see the bedrooms?"

The glint in his eye told her what he had in mind. Before she could speak, he kissed her, long and hard, making her breath hitch in her throat. She broke from him, her pulse racing, and put her fingers to her lips, then twisted out of his embrace.

"I don't think I should take you on a tour."

"Maybe not yet. Maybe it's too soon. For you, that is," he said, his eyes glowing.

"That's it, exactly. Too soon."

He kissed her hand, glanced at his watch, and headed for the door.

"Crikey, it's late. Thanks for showin' me this place. Like something from a museum."

"It is. Thanks for breakfast."

"We'll do it again before you go," he said, his hand on the doorknob.

She brushed his lips with hers, then shut the door behind him. Leaning back against it, she let out a breath.

"Laura Fleming, you goody-two-shoes. You're breaking all the rules. Wouldn't Mr. Banley be shocked if he knew?" She chuckled and headed for the kitchen. Time to bake something for the carolers who were arriving tonight.

She wrote out an invitation for her friend and Banley's neighbor, Ellen, to join her for dinner and caroling. *You already broke the damn rule. What's one more person gonna hurt?* She donned an apron and pulled out the flour canister. Jasper entered, meowing. He rubbed against her legs and she gave him the treat he'd been angling for. At the push of a button, the radio played Christmas music.

Episode Eight

ROME, ITALY

In a suite in the Grand Hotel Via Veneto in Rome, Craig stood and stretched his arms to the ceiling. His stomach rumbled so he raised his gaze to the clock. It was only four, and dinner wouldn't be until eight.

"Damn!" Craig made a face as his stomach protested the lack of food a second time.

"Don't get testy. I've ordered a snack," George said.

Craig smiled. "I should have known."

At the knock on the door, George rose to answer it. A waiter entered with a tray of Italian pastries and rich, dark coffee. A pitcher sat on the tray.

"Real cream?" Craig raised his eyebrows.

"Wouldn't have anything else."

The two men had been working since nine. They had amassed all the figures from the year and prepared the coming year's goals. Craig grinned.

"Great work and real cream. This is a good day."

George begged off refreshments and headed toward his bedroom to take his afternoon nap. Craig poured the coffee and took two cannoli off the plate.

"I wonder what our little Cinderella's been up to," he said to no one. He figured at ten in the morning, she'd be in. With a

28

grin, he set his phone on the table and tapped on the security app. The first room to come up was the living room. No one there. He checked every room. Emitting a sigh, he took another sip and picked up another sweet.

Clicking back to start, he saw the front door open. A smile graced his face. Then he saw it. His eyes widened. He rubbed them and looked again. Then blinked, rubbed, and looked again. No, he wasn't mistaken. There was a man following Laura into his home. A man!

Every curse word he knew came flying out of his mouth at record decibels. George raced into the room.

"What is it? What's the matter?" the older man said, suppressing a yawn.

"She did it! She did it! She broke the rule!" Craig lunged forward from his chair to his feet. He paced across the room. "Damn it! Damn it! She did it."

"What?"

"She brought a man home. A man!" Craig picked up a cloth napkin and threw it down on the table. He returned to his phone and hit *play*. There was no sound, but they saw Sean kissing her.

Fury flew through Craig's veins. He called her every vile name in the book while stomping across the floor. She was there with a man. Tired out by his anger, he slumped into a chair. Miss Laura Fleming was kissing a man in *his* house. And it wasn't him. He dropped his head to his hands. It wasn't him. It would never be him.

Episode Nine

LAURA SLIPPED A HANDWRITTEN note under the front door of the next townhouse. Ellen lived there. She'd met her the first year she house-sat for C.W.

She remembered the jaundiced eye the older woman shot at her and the third degree. Her pointed questions had flabbergasted Laura. No, she wasn't having an affair with that old man. Goodness gracious! How could anyone even ask?

But she and the older woman had met again and again in passing. Ellen had invited Laura in for afternoon tea. Ellen and her husband Bill had a wonderful housekeeper who was a talented baker. The three had enjoyed a delicious meal and conversation.

The next year, Laura discovered that her friend's husband had died. Ellen had been devastated. They had been married since "the beginning of time" as Ellen had said. Laura had invited Ellen to join her for breakfast out. The new widow had spent most of the year inside. But Laura had coaxed her to venture out to a small restaurant.

One night they dined together and listened to the carolers from Ellen's balcony. The singers performed every year from the museum's park across the street. They had shared hot toddies, and she had listened to Ellen recount past holidays with Bill, and their children.

This year, Ellen was using a cane. But at Laura's invitation, she managed to hobble up the steps anyway. The young woman figured a next-door neighbor would be an okay visitor.

"I've always wanted to see C.W.'s place," she said, slowly crossing the threshold.

"Well come on in. I baked cookies this morning."

"What kind?"

"Molasses and chocolate chip.

"My favorites," Ellen said, grinning.

Laura returned the smile. Her heart warmed to be able to make her friend happy. She closed the door against the cold and showed her into the living room. A tray with an antique porcelain pot and two cups and saucers sat on the gracious coffee table. Two plates of cookies flanked it.

Ellen sat on the sofa, resting her cane against the arm. She gazed all around the room.

"So, this is what that old skinflint C.W. spent his money on!"

"He's stingy?" Laura poured two cups, handing one to Ellen, who added sugar and cream.

"Oh yes. Notorious tightwad. What a piker! That's why he never married. No woman could stand it. Knowing he had such a big bank balance, yet holding on to it tight. He'd never wine and dine his lady friends in the best restaurants. Always used coupons and took them to cheaper places, taking advantage of saving every penny."

"Did you ever date him?"

"For a very short time. His cheapness ticked me off, too! Then I met Bill. He was a true gentleman and generous to a fault." She sighed.

"I'm so glad," Laura said, touching her friend's arm. She scowled at a smiling oil portrait of the old gent.

Ellen spied it and stuck out her tongue. "Old bastard," she muttered.

Laura was shocked to hear that word from her very proper friend.

"Now, what time are the carolers due tonight?" the older woman asked.

Episode Ten

ELLEN PICKED UP A COOKIE. Her sharp eyes stared straight at Laura.

"This is your third year coming here. The thrill must have worn off by now. Tell me the real reason you keep fleeing your home at Christmas." She sat back, chewing, waiting for a response.

Laura stiffened. Once she set foot in this mansion, her troubles melted from her mind.

"Who wouldn't jump at the chance to spend a few weeks in a palace like this and get paid for it?" Laura swallowed, praying her friend would buy it.

"The first year? I could see it. Maybe the second. But the third?" Ellen cocked an eyebrow. "Come on, fess up."

Laura shrugged. Telling her the truth couldn't hurt, could it?

"Okay. It's kind of a long, complicated story."

"We have at least an hour before the carolers arrive. I'm not going anywhere."

"I was married early, right out of college. To one of my professors. Ruger was his name."

Ellen leaned forward a degree or two.

"Go on."

"My father died when I was eight. We had been very close. His death was a huge loss to me. My mother remarried a Swiss

33

man. We moved to Geneva and she had two more children. By the time I was eighteen, I realized there wasn't room there for me anymore. So, I went off to college."

"And met this professor?"

"Yes. Before he died, my father put a large sum of money in a trust for me. I couldn't touch it until I was twenty-five."

Ellen picked up a molasses cookie but maintained eye contact.

"The marriage had been a bad idea. Ruger, ten years older than I, was controlling. Sometimes he was violent. I left him before I turned twenty-five."

"Aha! The money."

Laura nodded. "Right. He'd married me with an eye to getting his hands on my inheritance. He fought me on the divorce, but I got it anyway. He had hit me twice, and I had called the police, so he couldn't stop my leaving him."

"An abusive man? How awful, my dear," Ellen said, clasping her friend's hand.

Laura choked for a moment. "It was. It was devastating."

"But you seem to have recovered."

"I did. But when I got the money, Ruger started coming around. He said I owed him and he wanted at least half."

"Half? Some nerve. I hope you told him off."

"I did, sort of. Then he started harassing me on the job. I quit and started teaching my writing courses online from home."

"Did that work?"

"I put lots of locks on the doors and installed a security system. Still, I was afraid to go out for a long time. Then things got better. He left me alone."

"That's good."

"Until three years ago. He'd have time off at Christmas. You know, school break. And he had some gambling debts. He'd bang on my door. Scared me. So, when my friend, who knew about Ruger, told me about this house, I jumped at the chance."

"I guess he can't find you here."

"Nope. Thank God." Laura blew out a breath. "And I took out an order of protection."

"That's a good thing."

"Yes, but I'm not sure it applies here."

"What about your family? Your mother and stepsiblings?"

"They have a life of their own. They're still in Switzerland. I talk to my mom on the phone twice a year."

"I'm so sorry," Ellen said, patting Laura's hand.

"It's okay. I'm alone, but I don't mind. I get to go on adventures, like this one." She glanced at the ornate ceiling and the artwork on the walls. "Spending Christmas in this mansion, I love it."

"You're a brave girl. I'm glad you come."

"Me, too. Someday it'll be over. The old man'll die and leave this to a relative. They'll probably sell it and make a ton of money."

"Oh, I doubt that. Young Mr. Craig seems to like it here, well enough."

"Young Mr. Craig?"

"The old bastard's nephew."

"He lives here?"

"Yes. And a mighty fine neighbor, too. Always bags his trash. Says 'hello' on the street."

"Is he married? Does he have children?"

"Oh, no, my dear. He's quite single. And a fine catch, too. You can see how handsome he is in that picture."

Laura sensed heat in her cheeks and turned away. Young Mr. Craig? She had no idea. That changed everything.

"Where is he now?" Laura asked.

"Traveling, I hear. I think he likes the skiing crowd in Switzerland, this time of year."

"Oh."

"That's why you're hired. So, he can go gallivanting around, it seems."

"I see. That's fine. I'm glad to be here."

"Me, too, dear," Ellen said, patting her hand.

Episode Eleven

LAURA WRAPPED A SCARF around her neck. The night was clear and cold. She'd dragged the smallest chair she could find out onto the tiny terrace that overlooked 81st Street and the Theodore Roosevelt Park, which belonged to the American Museum of Natural History.

She spread a blanket on the chair and Ellen sat down. Then the two women wrapped the fleece around the older woman's legs.

"Ah, much better." Ellen nodded.

Laura retrieved two hot, spiked ciders. She stood next to Ellen, sipping the beverage, and watching the carolers assemble. The drink warmed her insides as she waited for the singing to begin.

They started with *Carol of the Bells*, one of Laura's favorites.

"Marvelous," Ellen whispered.

This ritual had warmed her heart every year, but not today. Standing against the wind, she shivered as cold penetrated her bones and her heart. Resting her hand on her friend's shoulder while listening to the lovely carols, loneliness engulfed Laura. She had dreamed of snuggling into the embrace of a handsome, sexy man, the love of her life, while holiday music washed over her.

She had wished for a heart brimming with excitement, await-ing his delight at each gift she gave, to feel the warmth of his touch, his hand holding hers, or his arm around her shoulders. To hear their voices raised together in song as their hearts joined in love were her most ardent desires. Laura sighed.

That is what she had asked Santa Claus for this year; the gift of true love. Santa hadn't been listening and it didn't look like that would be in her stocking anytime soon.

When she had first come to babysit the mansion, she had been breathless at the chance to stay in such a grand home. To call this luxurious place hers, even for a few weeks had been a thrill beyond imagination, one that had filled her dreams for weeks.

Now she had become comfortable living here, in every as-pect except one. She wanted to share it with a man. A loving, de-voted, funny, attractive man. But there was no one.

The picture of C.W. and his nephew had intrigued her. Not the old gent, but the younger version, was quite attractive. She had wondered where he was.

Finding out he lived here had sent a tingle up her spine. Of course, she didn't know what kind of person he was, but maybe her dreams could include staying here with him?

She shook her head. What a preposterous idea! What would a scion of such a wealthy family want with the likes of her, a no-body who had done nothing in life? Perhaps she shouldn't come back next year to the cream-colored house on the West Side?

It had been her escape, a chance to leave home for Christmas and salvage something bright and beautiful about the season. She hadn't heard from Ruger in six months and considered herself well rid of him. But the townhouse, oh how she ached to stay, become its mistress. That'd never happen.

Laura sighed again, and squeezed Ellen's hand. The rheumy, blue eyes glanced at her. Would her friend still be here next year? Perhaps not. That would make it harder to return.

She'd make the best of being here this year, then find another way to have a Christmas wish come true next year. Dreaming was one thing, but yearning was quite another. She rubbed her jacket above her heart. Then she raised her voice with Ellen's to sing *Silent Night*.

Episode Twelve

CHECKING ON LAURA FLEMING had become a nightly activity for Craig Banley. He and George would sip an evening brandy while Craig studied the screen. He saw her let Ellen in the house.

"She's done it again! Let in a stranger," Craig said, his mood darkening.

"Ellen Trabner is not exactly a stranger," George pointed out.

"Well, maybe not. But she's broken the rule a second time!" Craig pushed to his feet and paced. "This girl is a renegade. Can't obey the rules. Who knows how many undesirables she's had in the house?"

"You're overreacting, Craig."

"You think so? She signed a contract."

"What is it about this girl that upsets you so?" George sat forward in his seat.

"Nothing. Nothing about her at all. She's simply the house-sitter. And she signed a contract. And there are rules and she's broken them."

"Come now, Craig. You sound like a child." George raised his glass.

Craig poured another snifter from the bottle on the coffee table. "I am not. I'm just asking her to abide by the rules."

George laughed. "Really? Maybe we should return early so you can tell her yourself?"

The younger man stopped in his tracks. "Now that's an excellent idea, George! We'll arrive early. Take the little liar by surprise. Throw her out on her ass, too."

"And a fine ass it is, I'd say. Although I haven't even seen her in the altogether, like you did," George commented.

Craig's face colored. "That was a mistake."

"Does she know you're spying on her?"

"I'd think any intelligent person could see the cameras all over the place," Craig said, taking a swig.

"Really? I thought they said they'd gone out of their way to hide them."

"Well, maybe they did. So what? She shouldn't be breaking the rules," Craig said, lifting his chin.

"And she shouldn't be undressing in the bedroom, either?" George cocked an eyebrow.

"That's different."

"Really? How? And when she finds out, she'll probably call the police and accuse you of peeping," George said, stifling a smile.

Craig paled. "You're not going to tell her, are you?"

George leaned forward, placing his hand on the younger man's arm. "She's a lovely young woman. She's all alone at the holiday, Craig. How can you go home and toss her out? What a heartless thing to do. And it's Christmas. Where's your humanity?"

Craig stared at his thumbs. "I suppose you're right. But she's not alone. She had a man in there. It's just a matter of time before he comes to spend the night."

George raised his eyebrows. "You may be right about that."

"He's beat my time with her. She kissed him. Obviously, she likes him. Next step—bed." Craig's voice grew smaller.

"Then perhaps we'd better return sooner rather than later," George said.

"What's the point?" Craig sat back on the sofa and drained his glass.

"No Banley gives up without a fight. What would C.W. say?"

"He'd say I'm a pussy. I should get in there and stake my claim."

"Do you have a claim?"

"No. But neither does he, or he'd have spent the night," Craig said.

"I'll get on it tomorrow."

Craig shot the older man a quizzical glance.

"Changing the flights. We need to finish up here and get home, right?"

"Oh. Yes. Right."

George bid him goodnight and headed to his bedroom. Craig stood at the window, looking down on Rome. Could he finish his business in a few days and wing back to New York ahead of schedule? His brow furrowed. And if he did, what would he say to Laura Fleming, anyway?

Episode Thirteen

THE SUN WAS BRIGHT but brought no warmth to the chilly December air. Ellen's family had arrived for the holiday. Laura had volunteered to take her granddaughter on a walking tour of Fifth Avenue right after lunch.

After feeding Jasper, Laura brought her coffee into the living room and perused her mail. Marla, her friend in the Pine Grove post office, had forwarded her a stack of cards and solicitations. Laura hadn't wanted to miss the cards and letters she'd receive from old college friends this time of year.

Sunlight poured in through the front windows as there were no skyscrapers across the street to block it. The room warmed enough so that she didn't have to light the fire. She opened her laptop and hit play. Joyous sounds of the season from her Christmas playlist filled the room.

Jasper joined her, finding the perfect spot on a generous cushion bathed in sunlight. He sat and cleaned his paws, then his face for a bit, before curling up and drifting off. Laura hummed along to the cheerful songs as she ripped open envelope after envelope. Some notes made her laugh, others made her tear up. She missed her friends. It wasn't a huge circle, but she had joined a sorority and still kept in touch with about a dozen of her sisters.

At noon, on the button, the knocker drew her attention to the door. She let Linette Trabner in.

"Wow! This place is a whole lot fancier than Grandma's," the fifteen-year-old said.

"It's elegant, isn't it?" Laura said, zipping up her down jacket.

"Is this yours?"

"Oh, no. I wish. But no. I'm just the house-sitter."

"Oh." The girl nodded.

Laura slipped her camera phone into her pocket, petted Jasper goodbye, and opened the door.

"Where are we going?"

"I thought we'd take the subway down and start at Lord & Taylor's windows. Those are always wonderful. Then stroll up Fifth Avenue. There's so much to see."

"You know your way around," Linette said.

"After three years, I should."

They spent the most time at the Lord & Taylor windows that depicted the holiday in the 1600s, 1700s, 1800s, and 1900s. Each scene had moving figures, dressed in the fashions of the times.

They passed so many sights, Rockefeller Center, St. Patrick's Cathedral, Tiffany's, Cartier's, Victoria's Secret. They stopped at each one to take pictures and remark on the decorations, each more elaborate than the one before.

When they hit Central Park, a bench provided a place to stop and rest. Laura bought hot chocolate and hot dogs. Laura's cell rang. She made a face but checked the screen. It was Marla from Pine Grove.

"Merry Christmas, Marla. What's up?"

"Bad news, I'm afraid."

"What?" Laura straightened in her seat.

"The post office was broken into."

"That's a shame. Did they steal people's Christmas presents?"

"Nope. Nothing was taken," Marla said.

"Oh?"

"I was surprised. But your change of address card was sitting out on the counter."

Laura's pulse kicked up.

"I never leave those out. Someone must have taken it down."

"Oh, shit."

"Yeah. That's exactly what I said."

"Ruger." Laura's mouth went dry.

"I think so. I called the police. They went to his home, but there was no answer. Just thought you should know. I gotta go. Got customers. Merry Christmas, Laura."

Episode Fourteen

SATURDAY NIGHT, LAURA joined Ellen and her family for the Christmas carol sing-along concert at the church on Broadway. It was cold and windy. She bundled up, and wrapped her homemade scarf around her neck and face.

Laura loved to knit. She had knitted a scarf for C.W. and left it under the tree the previous year. This time, she'd made a hat to go with it, as well as other gifts. Tonight, she'd be going out with the Trabners. She forced thoughts about Ruger out of her mind. Surely it was all a coincidence, the post office break-in and her change of address card?

It was Christmas and she refused to come out of her fairytale to face the harsh reality of him. As long as she was in the house, she was safe. She silently thanked God and C.W. for the security system. She fed Jasper and headed for the front door, locking it behind her. If Ruger showed up, he'd find an empty house and never know where she'd gone. Comforted by that thought, she smiled as she headed next door to join her friends.

The giant, electrified snowflakes, strung over Columbus Avenue, created holiday cheer. One-by-one, the Trabner family exited the house. Laura, Ellen, her son, his wife, and children huddled together as they strolled west. First floor apartments in townhouses had Christmas trees in their windows. Laura marveled at how differently each family had decorated their tree.

Chatter of news of the year past occupied the group, turning Laura's attention away from the wind biting at her nose and cheeks. Mark Trabner was a forever cheerful guy. Mandy, his wife was a bit rotund and warm. They folded Laura into their family with ease. She smiled and listened, flattered to be accepted. This was the epitome of Christmas.

The old church was charming. The high, domed ceiling was painted with a religious scene. The cream-colored walls were immaculate, complementing the rich patina of the old wooden pews. The seats were filling fast, but the family managed to find a section where they could sit together.

After a few words from the pastor, the orchestra tuned up and the singing began. Laura learned from the program that the musicians were volunteers from Julliard, the famous music school. The church traded practice space for two annual concerts. There were strings, piano, woodwinds, and even a trumpet and trombone.

Laura raised her voice in song, grateful to be there, and filled with Christmas spirit. They started with *Adeste Fideles*, then on to *It Came Upon A Midnight Clear*. She knew song after song, without needing the songbook. Happiness filled her heart. Ellen squeezed her hand and they exchanged smiles. The concert finished with the *Hallelujah Chorus* from Handel's *Messiah*.

As they walked home, a shadow moving under the grand, circular steps up to her front door caught Laura's eye. Ruger? A mugger?

"I didn't eat much dinner, Ellen. I'm going to leave you and grab a quick bite at McGinty's," Laura said, stopping.

"We have food, dear. Why don't you come and join us?"

"I'd like to wish Sean a Merry Christmas," Laura said.

Ellen nodded. "I see. Okay. I get it. Thank you for joining us. Have a good night." Ellen patted her friend's hand and shot her a knowing look.

Laura blushed. *Let her think whatever she wants. I need to be safe.* She crossed the street and headed up toward the bright lights of the bar.

Episode Fifteen

"MISS LAURA FLEMING!" The call came from behind the bar.

She looked up to see Sean McGinty's handsome face smiling at her.

"Belly up to the bar lady. Whatcha havin'?" Sean swiped a rag over the surface of the wood counter.

The buzz of chatter forced Laura to lean in closer to hear him.

"What's your pleasure?" The barkeep's gaze warmed as it connected with hers.

The place was packed, not an empty table and just two seats at the bar begging for a customer. She slid her rump up on the stool and put her elbows on the bar.

"What do you suggest?"

"Don't be sayin' something like that. What I want has nothing to do with alcohol," he said, merriment twinkling in his eyes.

She sensed heat in her cheeks. He was flattering and so attractive. Why was she holding out? She couldn't come up with one good reason.

"On a cold night like this, might I suggest a hot, buttered rum? Or maybe mulled wine?"

"Mulled wine sounds perfect!"

"First one's on the house," he said, ladling a mugful and placing it in front of her.

"Now, Sean, you don't have to do that."

"Can't a gentleman buy a lady a drink?"

"I suppose."

The chill of seeing the shadowy figure near the house dissipated as the beverage warmed her bones. She'd stay here, under Sean's wing, until it was safe to return. How long would that be? She had no idea.

She ordered a burger and a side salad. The wine was so delicious, she finished her first mug quickly.

"Free refill for you, tonight," he said, taking her cup. "So, what brings you out on a cold night to such a noisy place?"

"Concert at the church," she replied, taking a sip.

"And then here?"

Should she tell him the truth? She wavered, the words stalled on her tongue wouldn't move.

"A secret, now?" he asked, his brows raised.

"There was someone lurking under the stairs."

Sean's eyes widened. "A mugger? I'll make fast work of 'im." His Irish eyes flashed.

She placed her hand on his arm. "I don't think it was a mugger. I think it was my ex."

He smiled. "I'm a champion at getting rid of exes. Wait until we close? I'll take you home."

Letting out a breath and nodding, she hoped he'd offer. Sean placed her food in front of her. Suddenly hunger took over. As Laura tucked into her food with renewed appetite, she watched Sean man the bar. He seemed to be everywhere at the same time, mixing drinks, then taking money. Relieved to have Sean as her knight in shining armor, Laura relaxed.

Her pulse kicked up a notch as she watched him work. Rolled up sleeves revealed his strong forearms. She yearned to have them around her again. Sean worked fast but with a smile, shooting his sexy grin at women from one end of the bar to the next. Surely he could keep her safe from Ruger. But who would keep her safe from Sean?

Episode Sixteen

MARSEILLE

Craig and George unpacked their bags in the luxurious Le Petit Nice on the rue de Braves in Marseille.

"I hear the food here is excellent," George said.

Craig settled on a modern sofa facing a huge window with a view of the sea. The rooms were spare but luxurious and attractive. The bathroom was sinful, with a tub large enough for two, giving Craig ideas.

"Such a romantic hotel you picked, George. It's kind of depressing to be here with you. No offense."

"None taken. I get your point. Might be a tad more exciting if Miss Laura Fleming was here."

At the mention of her name, Craig picked up his phone.

"Haven't checked on her today?" George cocked an eyebrow.

"No, I haven't. And after she had that girl in yesterday."

"But only for a few minutes."

"Yes, but that was the third time she broke that rule."

"May I?" George asked, sitting down.

"Of course."

The men perused the house, but there was no activity. When Craig moved to her room, they could see the outline of calves and feet under the covers in her bed.

"She's still asleep," George observed.

"Let's look around. See what mess she's created," Craig said.

George shot his boss a dirty look.

"Okay, okay. The house is hers for now. It won't matter." Still the younger man moved around, going from room to room.

"Wait. Stop," George said. "Are those presents under the tree in the living room?"

"Yes. She leaves stuff there every year."

"She leaves presents for you?" The older man's eyebrows shot up.

"She thinks I'm C.W. She leaves stuff for him. Old man stuff."

"Like what?"

"A scarf. I think she knit it herself."

"You mean that charcoal gray one you wear all the time?"

Craig sensed heat in his face. "Yeah."

"And what do you do?"

"I have Maeve leave stuff. She cooks and leaves a few things in the freezer so Miss Fleming can eat if she arrives late. We leave the fridge stocked with milk, eggs, beer, wine, and chocolates."

"You do?"

Craig nodded. "Didn't at first. But when I saw the things she left for me, well, I talked to Maeve and she suggested those things."

"Nice idea. Makes her feel welcome."

"I suppose."

"I'd guess you look forward to unwrapping her gifts, too?"

Craig stared at his hands for a moment. He looked sheepish. "I suppose it's silly, but I do."

"Those are the only presents you get this time of year, aren't they?"

The younger man nodded. "C.W. and I stopped exchanging gifts when he moved to Denver."

"Such a shame," George said, shaking his head.

"A few trifles. So what?"

"It's not about the stuff. It's about the time. Someone thinking about you."

"Her molasses cookies are the best."

"She leaves cookies?"

"A nice tin, filled."

"My, you are a lucky man."

Craig turned his gaze to the sea. There was a knock on the door and a pot of hot chocolate and two cups arrived, along with a basket of fresh croissants. As the men sipped their refreshment, Craig's thoughts turned to Laura.

"Her cookies would be perfect right now."

"Too bad she's not here," George replied.

Episode Seventeen

LAURA TURNED UP THE Christmas music. She pulled out a fresh box with new ornaments in it. C.W. kept adding to his collection. Pleased that he'd put a tree in her room this year, she provided one for the den. The room was dwarfed by the gigantic television screen. Perhaps the old guy and his nephew plopped down there with a pizza to watch football on Sundays?

Laura hummed along as she began to dress the tree. This year, she'd made an extra gift for him. She'd taken an online knitting class and made him a pair of socks. She'd measured his shoes for size. She draped the lights on the evergreen quickly, then began with ornaments. She finished with a touch of tinsel high enough to be out of Jasper's reach.

Chuckling to herself about the old gent finding a gift where he least expected it, she nestled the package under the tree, up against a box of special chocolates made by a small company two towns away from Laura's home. The first year she brought those, C.W. sent a glowing email.

Even though he was a fabulously wealthy man, Laura knew that Christmas was about getting a thoughtful gift from someone who spent some time thinking about the present and the person who would receive it. During the year, she kept an eye open for unusual things she thought C.W. Banley might appreciate.

As the song *I'll Be Home for Christmas* began, there was a sharp rap on the front door. The loud, angry knock startled her. Fear spiked inside as she tiptoed toward the front of the house. Breathing in short spurts, she sidled slowly up to the peephole. Ellen certainly wouldn't make such a bang. Even Sean had more finesse. Her heart pounded as she raised her eye to take a look.

The sight of Ruger confirmed her worst fears. He stepped up close, putting his eye on the other side of the spy hole. Laura jumped back, gasping. She covered her mouth with her hand, her eyes wide. What could she do? Ignore him, that's what.

"Laura! I know you're in there. Answer this door!"

Episode Eighteen

THE TWO MEN TOOK A break at five. A snack arrived in their suite and they put their papers aside.

Craig picked up his phone. "How can I get sound outta this thing?"

"Now you want to listen to her, too?"

"Look, she's in the kitchen. Baking. She looks like she's maybe singing. Dancing, too."

"So she is," George said, leaning over to gaze at the phone.

"I want to hear what she hears."

"Maybe Christmas music."

"Probably."

"When was the last time you listened to Christmas music, Craig?"

He shrugged. "Dunno. Since C.W. handed me the business, I haven't had much time for holidays."

"But music is different. You can listen while you work."

"I suppose. After Mom died, I stopped celebrating holidays."

"That's a shame."

"What's the point of celebrating alone?"

"With your resources, you could make Christmas a much happier time for a lot of people, including yourself."

"You mean buy Christmas cheer?"

"I mean donating money, or hosting a party for underprivileged kids."

Craig nodded. "I do give money. About the party, I suppose I could. Still be hard to do by myself."

"Maybe Miss Fleming would help you?"

Craig's face flushed. "Can you get sound on this thing?"

"Give it to me." The older man took the phone and fooled with it for ten minutes. "There. I think I found the place for sound."

"Good," Craig said, turning up the volume.

"Ah, one of my old favorites, *Rockin' Around the Christmas Tree.*"

Craig watched the lovely Laura scoop up globs of dough and put them on a cookie sheet.

"Looks like she's found a way to celebrate alone. Maybe she'd give you some advice," George remarked, a twinkle in his eye.

"Stop playing Santa, George. You don't have the belly for it."

Craig could almost smell the cookies as they baked. When she left the room, he switched around until he found her in the den.

"She's bought a small tree for the den."

"Craig, we've got work to do," George said

"Just a few more minutes."

His gaze followed her as she trimmed the tree and tucked a small package underneath. His heart swelled with a longing to join. He'd not thought of putting a tree in the den, but Laura had found the perfect one and decorated it in blue and silver.

"She thinks I won't find that little package she hid under the tree. But I'm way ahead of her."

"You're cheating. Spoiling the surprise."

Craig frowned. "I suppose you're right."

As he was about to turn off the video, he heard a loud banging.

Episode Nineteen

CRAIG'S MUSCLES TENSED as he watched Laura peek through the peephole, then cower.

"George!"

The older man glanced up from his work.

"George, come, quick!"

When he sat down next to Craig, the younger man pointed.

"Look! She's scared. Someone's trying to break in. We should call the police."

"You're overreacting."

"No, look. See? She's hiding."

"She's standing with her back to the door."

"Look at her hands," Craig said, pointing.

"So?"

"She's obviously terrified. Don't you see it?"

"Frankly, no. I see that you're determined to be a knight on a white horse or some such nonsense. It's ridiculous. Why don't you simply ask the poor woman out on a date when we get back?"

"Have you changed our reservations?"

"Yes. But I couldn't get anything earlier than five days from now."

"Five days! She could be dead by then."

"Calm down! Honestly, for such a level-headed business-man, you've gone off the deep end for this young woman."

He pondered George's words. Was the old man right? Was Craig creating a fantasy because he'd been alone for so long? He watched as Laura pulled her arms close, and a face appeared at the window.

"She's trapped. He's at the window. If she moves, he'll see her."

Both men listened. They heard Ruger's command.

"Now do you believe me? He's threatening her. She knows him and she's not opening the door. This isn't good. Isn't good at all." Craig shook his head.

"Damn! You may be right," George said, leaning closer to the phone.

"Laura! You know what I want. My share. You owe me!" Came through to the men.

The banging on the door continued.

"Stop! You'll wreck the door! This isn't my house. Please."

"You want me to stop? Then let me in!"

They watched her turn and throw open the locks. The man pushed his way in.

"Face-to-face. Much better."

"Ruger, you have to go. I can't give you any money," she said, backing away from him.

"Yes, you can. I know you got your inheritance. And I want some. I was your husband. I'm entitled to half."

She gasped.

"But I'll settle for twenty grand."

"I haven't got that kind of money."

"Then get it. I know you can."

"I can't. I don't have much."

"Then give me what you have."

"No!" He slapped her hard across the face. Laura fell and Craig bolted up out of his chair.

"That dirty bastard," he muttered under his breath.

The man continued. "Shut up. Five days. I'll be back. That gives you plenty of time to get it. And if you don't have it," he said, walking over to the fine mantle in the living room, "then I'll just take some of this stuff. Antiques, I guess. They'll bring big bucks." He ran a finger down an old, stately, wood clock.

"This house isn't mine," she said rubbing her cheek. A tiny bit of blood trickled from her lip.

"So what? You've got the key. I need the money. And you owe me."

"I don't owe you anything. Get out. Don't you dare touch Mr. Banley's things. Get out!"

Jasper sauntered in. He stared and hissed, his fur raised.

"Get that animal away from me," Ruger spat at her.

"Leave!" Laura stood up.

"I'm going. But I'll be back."

She followed him to the door and locked it behind him. Then she fell against it and slid down to the floor, sobbing.

"George, start packing. We're going home," Craig said, shutting off the phone.

"But we can't get a reservation."

"We'll find a way. Laura's in trouble. Come on. Let's go."

Episode Twenty

LAURA CRAWLED TO THE kitchen and turned off the oven. She was through baking for the day. She pushed to her feet and headed for the bathroom. After splashing cold water on her face, she examined her injury in the mirror. It was already swelling and she could see the tinge of redness that would soon turn purple.

Back in the kitchen, she grabbed a liquor bottle with a shaking hand, and poured a glass of brandy. Then she retrieved two ice cubes, wrapped them in a dish towel, and applied them to her face. Christmas music played as she downed the beverage. Within a few minutes, she had calmed down enough to think.

Laura had to go to the police. Maybe to Sean, too. But what could he do? *Probably nothing.* He had a bar to run and couldn't be her protector whenever she snapped her fingers. The police would have to do. She stopped at McGinty's to get the address of the local police station.

"What happened to you?" Sean turned concerned eyes on her.

Laura explained. "Can you direct me to the nearest police station?"

"Your ex? If that bastard comes back, call me. I'll come over and break his face."

"Thank you," she said, patting his arm. "But I think I need the police."

She wrote down the address and headed out the door. Still shaky, she checked the street before leaving the bar. It was only three blocks to the station.

She met with an officer and told her story.

"Do you have an address for this guy? Do you want to file assault charges?"

"I don't know where's he's living now."

"Without an address, I can't pick him up. Here's my card. Call me if he shows up again."

Laura nodded.

"Oh, I'll ask our guys to drive by your place a couple of times in the next few days, in case he comes back. Where are you?"

She gave them C.W.'s address, thanked the officer, and tucked the business card in her pants pocket and left. Although Laura knew there was nothing more the police could do, disappointment mixed with fear in her chest. How could she call them if Ruger was inside with her?

Next stop—the bank. Yes, she had that much money and more. Her father had left her three hundred thousand dollars. She didn't make much teaching an online course and relied on the income she got from her few investments to pay her living expenses. Unfortunately, the bank told her it would take longer than three days to get the money. More like a week—they'd have to verify her identity with her bank and such. Seemed like there was much red tape connected with getting that much money in cash.

As she walked home, Laura pondered if Ruger would stop at twenty thousand. Why stop there? If she gave him the money, he'd surely come back again and again. What's to stop him? He'd bleed her dry, scaring her into anteing up. Now used to living alone, she rather liked the peace and quiet. With friends in Pine Grove, Laura attended community events, and had become a regular at the coffee shop. She even belonged to a book club. But today, being alone took on new meaning. The idea of living the rest of her life in fear and poverty terrified her. But what choice did she have?

Curled up on the floor, Jasper awaited her return. She sank down on the couch, and munched on a cookie, trying to figure out a way to set a trap for Ruger. She had to get him arrested if she wanted to live her life. It sure seemed easy enough to do on television and in the movies. Could she do what she saw on TV, week-after-week? Laura's brows knitted. She twisted one hand within the other. It couldn't possibly be that easy, could it?

"Jasper? What do you think? What should I do?"

He jumped up on the sofa, stretching out next to her.

Episode Twenty-One

CRAIG AND GEORGE STOPPED at the front desk.

"I need to get to Paris *tout suite*."

"The flights are booked. But there is a train."

"Two tickets, please. Right away."

While the manager checked on the tickets, George faced him.

"But we have no plane reservation for four more days."

"I know. But we can't change that sitting on our butts in the hotel. We need to be at the airport."

"I have no idea how that's going to do any good. It'll simply waste four days where we won't be able to get any planning done. And in the end, we'll just get on our scheduled flight anyway."

"You have no faith, George. We'll find a way. We have to. She needs us."

George cocked an eyebrow. "Us? You maybe. Certainly not me."

"Then I need you. Once we get to Paris, we'll stop at the bank. Where's the checkbook?"

George furnished the document and Craig filled it out and signed it.

"What's that for?"

"Bribes," Craig replied.

"I'm so sorry, sir. The fast train is booked. No tickets. There might be tickets on the regular train."

"How much cash do we have, George?"

The older man pulled out his wallet. "About fifteen hundred Euros."

"That should be enough," Craig said, then turned to the desk clerk. "Find me a car. It's worth a thousand Euros for the driver. We need to get to Paris right away."

"That's a very long trip, sir. At least seven hours by car."

"Dammit, I don't care!" Craig banged his fist on the desk. "This is a matter of life and death." He waved the money in front of the man. "And here's fifty for you, just for finding us the driver."

The man's eyes lit up. "Yes, sir. Life and death. We will stop at nothing." He scurried away.

"Are you sure?" George began.

Craig raised his palm. "Don't. We're doing this."

"If you say so. Seems like much ado about nothing. Maybe she should just give him the money?"

"Do you really think a violent man like that is going to stop at the money? He'll take everything in the house that he can carry and then kill her to leave no witnesses."

George rubbed his chin. "I never thought of that."

"It's up to us now. The police probably think she's some crazy woman. Besides, they can't do anything until that lunatic returns. By then, it'll be too late. I'm her only chance."

"When you put it that way, I see your point," George replied.

"Good, because we're going to move heaven and Earth to get there on time."

"*Messieurs, ici* Jean Paul. He's consented to drive you."

"Very good. George, get the bags. Here you go. Five hundred now and the rest when we arrive," Craig said, forking over the fee.

"*Bien sur. Allons-y!*" the Frenchman said, leading the way.

The doors slammed and the engine roared to life.

"At least we'll get a tour of the countryside," George said, sitting back in the small automobile.

"I've never had someone's life in my hands before." Craig stared out the window.

"Quite a responsibility."

"Scary as hell. We'll do it. We've got to."

Episode Twenty-Two

"WELL, JASPER, WHAT are we going to do now? Christmas is ruined." Laura stood in the kitchen, pouring herself a cup of coffee. The ginger-striped cat rubbed against her legs.

"I haven't forgotten you but coffee comes first." She took a sip then picked up the small can and popped open the tab. After dumping the kitty tuna in his dish, she lowered it to the floor. Jasper was there in a heartbeat.

She picked up a gingerbread cookie and plopped onto a chair. Laura had tossed and turned all night, trying to find solutions to the Ruger problem. If she gave him the money, would he go away or would he ransack Banley's house anyway? She'd bounced back and forth between her memories of Ruger as a decent sort when she had married him, and the greedy, cheating scoundrel he had become within the first two years.

If she gave him the money and he took a few things, then he'd leave, right? And she could call the police? She tugged on her lip with her teeth. He wouldn't harm her, would he? She'd be the only witness. Even though she didn't have his address, she knew he was the thief. A chill swept through her.

At dawn, Laura had decided that she had to roll the dice. If she gave him the money, there was a good chance he'd leave her alone. If she didn't, then for sure she'd end up badly.

She showered and dressed, playing Christmas music, trying to recapture the spirit. She'd resolved to finish her baking in the afternoon. *Ruger is not going to ruin my holiday! Who knows? Old C.W. might just stay home next year. That would make this my last time here.* She sighed.

After hitting the street, her nerves zoomed to high alert. Surely, Ruger wouldn't jump her in broad daylight, would he? She trembled a bit until she reminded herself that he was after the money. He knew she didn't have it yet and he'd wait. She bustled down the street to the nearest bank. Before she moved the money out of her Trusts Unlimited account, she had to make sure a local bank would cash the check.

She entered the Metropolitan Bank and headed for an officer. Laura said that she needed to cash a large check. The woman behind the desk explained that Laura would have to open an account first. It would take ten business days for a check that size to clear and the money to be available.

"What about a wire transfer?"

"That's different. If the money was wired in, it would be available the next day."

"Could I take it out as cash?"

"We frown on handing out that kind of cash. And if there was nothing left in the account, well, we're not comfortable with that either."

"Okay, so if I wired forty thousand and take out twenty, would that work?"

The woman nodded.

"How do I open an account?"

She spent the next two hours on her laptop and the phone wiring the money and assuring Trusts Unlimited that she was indeed Laura Fleming and that the transfer was on the up and up. Exhausted, she lay on the couch in the library, covered herself with a throw she'd made and gifted to C.W. two years ago and opened a book. Jasper meowed as he entered the room. He curled up next to her, purring. It wasn't long before Laura and the cat were asleep.

When she awoke, she padded downstairs to the kitchen. On the way, Laura noticed a paper slipped under her door. She wondered if it was a Christmas card from Ellen, or Sean. She picked it up and read,

> *Instead of twenty, make it one fifty. Half of what you got and what you owe me.*

She gasped, tamping down the panic that coursed through her veins.

Episode Twenty-Three

CRAIG REROUTED THE driver to the bank. They made a withdrawal and then headed for the airport.

"I'm sorry, monsieur. There are no seats on any flights out for the next three days," said the woman behind the airline ticket counter. "It is the holiday."

"You don't understand. This is life and death. If we don't get there, a young woman is going to die," Craig said, his voice low.

"Monsieur, begging your pardon, but I hear that every day."

"This is real. I need your help."

"Sometimes a passenger is willing to give up a seat, for certain, compensation?"

"I'm offering five thousand Euros for two seats."

Her eyebrows shot up. "It certainly must be life and death. I'll make the announcement."

"Let's get a drink," George said, tugging on Craig's sleeve.

"But what if she finds someone while we're gone?"

"Miss, will you hold the seats for twenty minutes, if someone agrees to sell?"

She nodded.

"Come on, then."

Craig followed the older gentleman to the bar. They ordered brandy.

"And what if you save her? What then? Just curious," George asked.

"I have no idea."

"That's not good."

"First, we have to save her, George. Nothing else matters." Craig drained his snifter.

"I suppose. Perhaps she's the one?"

"Don't be ridiculous. I'm thirty-five, there is no 'one' for me."

"Just because you've slept your way through the Hamptons, Zermatt, and London, doesn't mean there isn't a girl somewhere for you. Maybe just not there."

Craig cracked a smile. "Only you could make me laugh at a time like this."

"Undoubtedly she'll be grateful."

"First, we have to win, then I'll worry about the rest."

An announcement, paging Craig Banley, came over the loudspeaker. George chugged his remaining drink and the men headed for the counter.

"This nice couple has agreed to your offer, Monsieur Banley."

"Excellent. When does the plane leave?"

"Tomorrow morning, eight o'clock."

Craig paid the older folks and thanked them profusely.

"Been a long time since I've heard of love called life or death, Mr. Banley." The man chuckled.

Craig didn't bother to correct him, simply took the ticket and, with George in tow, headed for a taxi.

"We'll stay at the hotel here."

Once they checked in, George ordered lunch from room service. Craig stretched out on the bed and picked up his cell. Before he tuned into the security camera, he turned to George.

"Arrange for two limos to meet us at Kennedy."

"Two?"

"One to take me to the house and the other to take you to the police station on 83rd Street."

"Oh, right." George opened the laptop.

Craig leaned back against the bed. He tuned in the security camera. "She's watching a movie. Probably a Christmas movie," he announced.

George stopped typing. "It's almost like being there with her. You could probably see the movie, too."

Craig gave a half-smile. *Almost isn't good enough anymore.*

Episode Twenty-Four

CHRISTMAS EVE, LAURA made a fire in the den, popped up a big bowl of popcorn, brewed a pot of tea, and settled down to watch *It's a Wonderful Life* for the millionth time. Jasper padded in after her. She plucked a treat from her pocket and rewarded the feline for his company. He jumped up on the couch and curled up next to her.

She drew a box of tissues near, knowing she'd need them for the movie, and her own predicament. After that note from Ruger, she'd panicked until she realized it was too late to get additional money. He'd have to settle for his original demand. Fear spiked through her. She'd called Sean, who couldn't talk but told her to call him if "that bastard" showed up again. His offer did little to calm her nerves. Jimmy Stewart's movie was a last resort. Soon she was engrossed in the story that had nudged her worries aside. The warmth of cat fur and the vibration of his purr against her leg helped relieve the tension.

She planned to open the few presents old C.W. had left for her, play her holiday songs, and finish baking tomorrow morning. She prayed that Ruger would not return.

The movie was long. After it ended, Laura yawned and dried her tears. As she undressed for bed, she picked up the small picture frame on the tiny desk in her room. There were pictures of C.W. and his nephew. One showed them on a boat, holding up their catches, another showed the men, much younger, in ski gear on a snowy slope. She wondered where the young man's family was—was C.W. his only relative?

No longer as sleepy as before, she decided to read. Her eyes scanned the four built-in, white pine bookshelves. All hardbound books, mostly thick thrillers, which did not interest her. Her gaze fell on a smaller one. Pulling up a stepping stool, she got close enough to read the title scratched in cursive. *The Banley Family: A History.*

She pulled the thin volume down and switched off the overhead light. Laura slipped into bed, pulled up the comforter, and cozied up to the bedside lamp. Running a tissue over the cover, she removed most of the dust, then opened it, gently. There was a dedication inside.

For my brother, Chester William Banley, head of our family since the death of our parents, Martha and Joseph W. Banley.

Chester? No. C.W.'s name is Craig. Right? Emails come from Craig W. Banley, don't they? She shook her head. If the old man, the old C.W., was Chester William Banley, then who was Craig Watson Banley? The nephew? That handsome man—could he be the C.W. Banley she'd been corresponding with?

Deep embarrassment heated her face. She switched out the light before reading more, too ashamed to continue. When she thought of the gifts she'd left for the "elderly" gentleman—and all along he'd been a young, handsome one. Geez, knitted socks? A scarf? A book on General George Patton?

She'd made a terrible mistake. Impulse gripped Laura, she turned on the light, threw down the bedclothes, and dumped her valise on the bed. Frozen in mid-step, she realized she couldn't leave. How could she leave the house unprotected with Ruger due back soon? Surely he'd take a hatchet to the door and steal everything he could carry. And who would feed Jasper?

She put the suitcase away. Curiosity piqued her interest. Here was a book that would tell everything, or she hoped it would. She climbed back into the comfortable bed and opened it again.

I keep this record for my beloved son, Craig Watson Banley, nephew to Chet Banley. Someday he will want to know where he came from and who he belonged to. This should give him all the answers.

Affectionately,
Mary Enright Banley

Laura turned the page carefully as the book was old. She read about Chet and Mary's hardscrabble existence in the hills of Sullivan County. Craig had been born out of wedlock. Chet had agreed to look after him while Mary went off to have a career or find a husband. The book was vague about her reason for leaving.

Things faltered after that. There were large chunks of time with no entries. Finally, Chet wrote:

It pains me to write of the passing of my sister, Mary. She went to meet her maker today. I am applying to officially adopt little C.W., as I call him. The boy shows great promise.

Six months later was the last entry:

I've been offered a good job on Wall Street in New York. I've sold my parents' farm. Little C.W. and I are moving to the big city. Guess I should call him Craig, as he's not so little anymore. He's as unruly and undisciplined as any fifteen-year-old. I'll get him on the right path for Mary. The boy and I

*have had many adventures and it's time to settle
into a steady life.*

*I regret that I don't foresee time to keep up with
Mary's family history here. It's time for me to
make money and raise the boy. So this will be
the last entry, unless the other C.W. chooses to
pick up the pen. Bless you, Mary. Thank you for
Craig. He's made a true man and father out of me.
Yours in good faith,
Chester William Banley*

Laura doused the light and closed her eyes. A young C. W. tripped through her dreams.

Episode Twenty-Five

ON CHRISTMAS MORNING, a light snow frosted the trees, shrubs, and the sparse grass. Jasper awoke first. He meowed in her face with his tuna breath. When she gagged and rolled over, he batted at her hair, getting his claws caught in it, screeching and pulling until she was screaming.

The pair padded downstairs, where Laura fed the feline, then put up coffee. She snapped on Christmas music and set about making the last batch of cookies. According to C.W., chocolate pixies, this current batch, were his favorites. A blush and a tingly feeling flushed through her when she remembered that C.W. was the handsome thirty-something man in the photo, not the old geezer.

While the last batch cooled by the open window in the back, Laura went upstairs to shower and dress. She returned to the kitchen to the sound of church bells. She hummed along with the music as she arranged cookies in two tins. She'd deliver one to Ellen, too.

She tied a ribbon on, included a card, and eased the festive package under the tree in her room. She wondered how long it would take him to go in there. A chill reminded her that she'd forgotten to close the window on the back porch, which meant the security system wasn't keyed on. When she opened the door a man's deep voice and large presence greeted her. The screen in the window had been cut.

"Ho, ho, ho, Merry Christmas. Do you have my money?"

Laura dropped the dishtowel she carried.

"What are you doing here?"

"I came for the money."

"I only have the twenty thousand. The bank is closed."

"Yeah, I know. So I'll take a few things to make up for it," he said, pushing past her, knocking her hard against the wall, smashing her elbow into the window sash. She winced.

"Please, Ruger. I have the money. Please don't take anything from Mr. Banley."

"Why not? He's got plenty. He won't miss a few things," Ruger stopped in the living room and eyed the antique mantle clock.

"Please, Ruger. He'll think I took it," she pleaded.

He laughed. "So what? I don't give a rat's ass what he thinks. First the money. Get it!"

He raised his voice, startling her.

"You heard me, go on!" He shoved her.

She fairly flew up the stairs. The phone! But it was in Mr. Banley's room, across the hall, and she spied Ruger watching her every step. Besides, sometimes the old man unplugged it when he went away. She had no time to connect it and call the police.

The thought of locking herself in her room tempted her. But she knew it would do no good. He'd simply break down the door or steal everything in sight. With trembling hands, she pulled the fat envelope from her purse and headed down the stairs.

As she got closer, he reached out and snatched the cash, then slapped her across the face. She lost her balance.

"What was that for?" She sat on the floor, rubbing her jaw.

"Just because I can," he spat at her.

Laura crawled to a corner and leaned against the wall. Her pulse beat wildly, adrenaline and fear pounded through her veins, yet she could find no escape. Plucking her cell phone from the pocket of her apron, she tried to dial Sean behind Ruger's back, but he turned too soon.

"What the hell are you doing?" Ruger hollered, kicking the phone from her hand. Her fingers stung where they had made contact with his shoe. She rubbed them against her leg.

"I'll take that." He stuffed her phone into his back pocket.

Tears started. She was doomed now.

"Don't think about leaving or screaming or anything. 'Cause I'll fix you good if you do." He unfolded a shopping bag he'd had stuffed under his arm. Closing his grubby fingers around the clock, he lifted it carefully and deposited it in the bag.

"Please, Ruger. Please, don't." She stood, tugging on his sleeve.

"Shut the eff up." He smacked her hard across the face and she flew into the wall.

CRAIG AND GEORGE SAT in first class. They watched the security video on his phone with growing alarm. Craig bit his lip.

"If he hits her one more time, I'm going to rip him to pieces."

"Steady. Don't do anything rash. He might have a gun."

"Hah! Look at the coward! Beating up a defenseless woman. If he has a gun, I don't see it."

They watched as Ruger opened the silver drawer in the dining room. Laura tugged on his arm and he sent her flying into a chair, knocking it over and lying flat on the floor, crying. Craig hissed.

"I'll kill him."

"Easy, Craig. You're unarmed."

"That's what you think."

George cocked a quizzical eye at him.

"I have a Taurus PT one-eleven handgun loaded with thirteen rounds. It's in the grandfather clock in the foyer."

"Ruger's a goner."

"That's what I figure. He just doesn't know it yet."

"But you're not a killer, you're a money man."

"Every man rises to the occasion to defend his woman."

"But she's not your woman."

"Not yet."

George smiled and shook his head. "Love is blind," he muttered to himself.

Episode Twenty-Six

"CRAIG AND GEORGE EXITED the plane first. They ran to the baggage claim. Two drivers holding signs with their names on them stood ready.

"Grab the bags and go straight to the police. Eighty-third Street, I believe," Craig said.

"Right."

Each man connected with his own driver. Craig jumped into the limo and slammed the door seconds before it sped away.

"There's five hundred in it for you if you can get to my house in ten minutes," he said to the driver.

"I'll do my best, buddy."

As the man leaned heavily on the gas, Craig turned his phone on and held his breath as he tuned in to the security system. Laura sat on the floor, watching Ruger fill a pillowcase with more silver. She cried some, wiping her cheeks with her hand. Craig's heart squeezed. He wanted to dry those tears and hold her close.

"Hurry, man!" he said.

The car surged forward, slipping into the left lane. The vehicle screeched to a stop in front of the cream-colored townhouse. Craig threw a fistful of bills at the driver and exited. He stood at the door, key in hand, watching on his phone as Ruger headed for the stairs. His heart pounded as he heard the intruder's heavy footsteps.

Craig waited until the man turned the corner, then slid the key into the lock slowly. He turned the tumbler and gently eased the door open. He saw the grandfather clock but checked his cell to see where Ruger was before entering. The evil man was upstairs in the master bedroom.

Craig ground his teeth before stepping into the foyer. He had to keep his emotions under control. If he gunned down an unarmed man, he'd surely go to jail. Taking a breath to steady his hand, he turned the tiny key sitting in the lock and opened the door to the clockworks. There on the shelf sat the weapon. Wrapping his sweaty fingers around the cold steel, he checked to make sure it was loaded, then flipped off the safety.

Craig tiptoed into the living room, startling Laura, who still sat on the floor.

"Who—?"

He motioned her for silence, placing his finger to his lips.

"Don't be afraid. I'm here to save you," he whispered, then flattened himself against the wall.

He thought he saw a brief smile pass over her bruised and bleeding lips. She had a black eye and a bruise on her neck and cheek. Her hands were red and one finger had dried blood on it. Anger piped through him. His hand trembled, and his finger tightened on the trigger.

A footfall on the stairs alerted him to Ruger's return. With both hands, he raised his weapon chest-high and held his breath. Craig had done plenty of skeet shooting but had never shot a man. One more glance at Laura gave him courage. Ruger lumbered into the living room.

"Stop right there!" Craig commanded.

Ruger turned and C.W. aimed at the man's heart, assuming he had one.

"What the...?"

"That's right. Put down the pillowcase and stand against the wall. Craig motioned with his gun.

"Who the fuck are you?"

"I'm Craig Banley. I own this house. The police are on their way. Stand still and you won't get shot."

A wicked smile crossed Ruger's face. "Why you fuckin' little wimp-ass. You can't stop me." He charged, and Craig fired. Once into the man's thigh.

"Try that again, and I'll aim higher," he said, pointing the barrel at the man's groin. Ruger cringed.

"You fuckin' shot me! I'm bleeding!" He threw an incredulous glare at Craig.

"And I'll do it again if you don't shut the fuck up."

A soft voice drew his attention. "You're Craig Banley? C.W. Banley?"

"At your service," he said, giving a short bow.

At that point, police barged in. While they took over, Craig stole over to Laura.

"Are you all right?" he asked, putting down the gun and offering his hand. He helped her up and she swayed against him. He caught her to his chest and picked her up, carrying her to the sofa. After setting her down, he kissed her forehead.

"Miss Fleming?" A burly policeman asked, notebook open and pen in hand.

A call for an ambulance went out and confusion reigned. Ruger was cuffed. Police photographed the scene and returned the Banley possessions to their rightful owner. They interviewed Laura and Craig, who flashed his gun permit.

The EMT suggested Laura go to the hospital for x-rays and to get stitches. A second ambulance arrived. The first took Ruger away and the EMT escorted Laura to the second.

"Do you want me to go with you?" he asked.

She nodded. "If you don't mind. I know you're a busy man and you've just come home," she rattled on.

He stopped her, placing his fingers over her lips. "I want to. Let's go."

Episode Twenty-Seven

AFTER BEING CHECKED out at the hospital, they went to the police station, where they gave statements. By the time they reached the Banley residence it was one in the morning. Craig reheated leftovers and they sat, sipping brandy, and eating.

"Not sure I should be drinking with all the painkillers I'm taking," she said. He was so handsome and well dressed. She sensed she looked terrible, her face bruised, her clothes wrinkled and bloody. Embarrassment tied her tongue.

"A little nip won't hurt. Help you sleep." He momentarily covered her hand with his.

"I'm so lucky you happened to return when you did."

Craig retrieved ice from the freezer. He put it in a towel and pressed it to her cheek and mouth. "Here. This should take down the swelling."

She thanked him and held the cold pack to her face. He looked away. Was it because of the way she looked? *That can't be it. He's looked right at me all night. Hmm. What did I say?*

"It is not a coincidence you came home this afternoon, is it?" The moment she said it, she regretted it. *What a stupid remark. He must think I'm an idiot.*

"Well, to be totally truthful, no, it wasn't." He fidgeted with a napkin.

"What do you mean?"

"Surely you realized when you saw the security system that it came with video protection, too?"

"Video?" *Is my brain not functioning on all cylinders or was he watching me through a camera?* She raised her gaze to the ceiling and spied a small device by the kitchen door. She gasped and dropped her fork with a clatter. She turned frightened, angry eyes to Craig.

"You've been watching me? The whole time?"

"It's not like that. It was a mistake, at first."

"At first? How long have you?" But she couldn't finish, hiding her face with her hands.

"Don't worry."

"In the bedroom, too?" She turned a horrified gaze to him.

Now it was Craig's turn to blush. "Only once. By accident. But I didn't do it again."

"There are laws about that sort of thing," her tone hardened.

"Not in your own house," he countered. "Look, it was an accident. I was simply testing the system to see if it was working. I'd had a break-in last summer. The system was new."

"And?"

"Well—" he stopped to take a breath, his face turning a deeper shade of red. "I liked what I saw."

"What?"

"I mean, I mean, you were beautiful and you baked and cooked. It was almost like I was here celebrating Christmas with you."

He paused, his gaze seeking hers, his eyes pleading. "Please don't be angry. If I hadn't been watching, you might be dead now."

"True," she said, her voice stone cold.

"When we saw his first visit, that was it. George and I packed up. We made plans to return, immediately."

"Why?"

"Because you were in danger. You can't pay off someone like him. You'd be a witness. He'd have to kill you."

She took a breath.

"We were in Marseille. I paid a huge amount in bribes to get driven to Paris and get a couple to give us their seats on the plane."

"You did?"

He nodded. "Every flight was booked."

"What were you thinking?" Her eyes widened.

"All I could think of was that I needed to save you. Lovely Miss Fleming. I had to."

"But you don't know me."

"Oh, but I do. For three years now. I know you're a giving person. Responsible. You take excellent care of my house and my cat. And you leave me presents. This year, I wanted to open them with you."

Her throat closed. She'd abandoned the idea of Prince Charming long ago. *I must be dreaming.* He stroked the back of her hand.

"Please forgive me."

She withdrew her hand and sat back.

"I know it's stupid, ridiculous. Insane. Totally. And I don't expect you to believe me."

"Yes, it is," she agreed.

"But I can't get you out of my mind."

Episode Twenty-Eight

LAURA PUSHED UP FROM the table and turned toward the stairs with Craig right behind her. She put her hand on the banister and her foot on the first step, then wobbled. He caught her. As the reality of the threat to her life sank in, she collapsed into sobs. Craig held her to him, stroking her hair until she quieted down.

"Shock. Come on," he said, lifting her as if she weighed nothing. He carried her up to her room, where he laid her gently on the bed, then handed her his handkerchief.

After removing her shoes and socks, he grabbed a neatly-folded throw and spread it over her. He kissed her forehead. "Sleep well, my Laura. You need rest."

He flipped off the light and stole quietly from the room.

Once she was alone, Laura fought sleep. Her heart did flip-flops. What of Craig Banley? Was he a peeping Tom? Was he her knight in shining armor? Was he simply a man who did the wrong thing and now was doing the right thing? Her head ached. She pushed the cover off and sat up. She'd never rest fully clothed. As she stripped off her pants and shirt, she thought about C.W. He'd moved heaven and Earth to get to her, to save her, and he didn't even know her. Well, maybe he did, a little. She had held a high opinion of him as a kind and generous man until the camera thing.

A war raged between her heart and her head. Her head preached caution, but her heart already believed. What could she do? After she crawled into bed, exhaustion claimed her, silencing her inner voices.

When she awoke, one look at the clock had her out of bed. She'd slept until two in the afternoon. What about Jasper? He must be starving. She pushed up out of bed, grabbed her robe and headed for the kitchen, moving slowly because everything ached.

The sound of Christmas music alarmed her. A deep, male voice, singing along, stopped her in the doorway. Her head was fuzzy. Had she been taking drugs? Then it all came back to her, in frightening detail. She clutched her robe to her body and stepped into the kitchen.

"Ah, there you are. Sleep well? Feeling better?" Craig's cheery voice greeted her. "Ham and eggs, coming up. Coffee?" He poured a mug and handed it to her.

"I'll pack up and be on my way tonight." She sipped the brew. Milk and a touch of sugar, just the way she liked it.

"No need to rush home. Stay. I can look after you."

"I can't impose. It's bad enough what Ruger did..."

"Stop!" He clapped his hand over her mouth for a moment before releasing her. "None of this was your fault. You've been injured. You need someone to take care of you. And that's me."

"But I can't."

"Yes, you can. And you will."

Jasper entered and rubbed against her legs, adding his two cents to the argument.

"Jasper wants you to stay, too."

She eased down into a chair and leaned over to pet the feline.

Craig tended the food and refilled his cup. The java lifted her spirits. The kitchen was warm and cozy. With C.W. moving about, waiting on her, it seemed like the best dream in the world.

He portioned out two plates and brought them to the table, then dug in with gusto.

"Never been much of a cook. But any idiot can do ham and eggs," he said, wolfing down a forkful.

"Delicious," she said, marveling at how good food could taste when someone else cooked it.

He placed his hand over hers.

"You've been through a traumatic experience. I want you to stay as long as you like. Stay for a month, two, or six. Don't go home to an empty house. You'll be safe here."

She met his gaze and believed every word. She did feel safe, then she mentally scolded herself for falling for his lines. They were lines, weren't they? What if they weren't? That was almost the scarier proposition.

"I shouldn't." But what did she have to rush home to?

"I want to get to know you better. Maybe we could have a future together?" He blushed and lowered his gaze to his plate.

Her heart squeezed to see this wealthy, powerful man so humble. *He's lonely!* The idea surprised and pleased her. Perhaps he needed her as much as she needed him? She cupped his cheek, feeling the scrape of his scruff against the pad of her thumb.

"That would be a dream come true," she muttered, almost as much to herself as to him.

His head snapped up, and he covered her hand with his, turning his face to press his lips against her palm.

"Beautiful, Laura."

"I'm not so very beautiful now, am I?" She gave a half-smile.

"You are to me."

Her heart thumped faster. "It would be hard to travel, looking like this. I might scare people. I'd be grateful if I could stay for a bit. Just until I look better."

"Stay as long as you like." He dropped her hand and returned to his food. "After breakfast, I'll make a fire and open your presents. Okay?"

When they finished, he cleaned up and laid a fire while she dressed. He went from tree to tree, snatching up the gifts from each. She stretched out on the sofa and he covered her with a blanket. The fire roared, sending soft, warm light across his features. She'd swear he was the handsomest man on Earth.

Christmas music played from his phone. With the impish grin of a small child, he tore the paper off each gift. They laughed over the "old geezer" ones she'd made when she'd thought he was his uncle. He handed her a long, thin box. Inside was a stunning gold bracelet. He fastened it around her wrist.

"I can't," she started.

"Shh. Wear it. It's beautiful on you."

She lay back against the cushions. The painkillers relieved her discomfort and her heart filled with joy. This was the Christmas of her dreams. Well, after the Ruger part. Craig sat on the sofa next to her and massaged her foot.

"Since you know so much about me, tell me about your life," she said, enjoying his tender touch.

"Where should I begin?"

"How about when you lived in Sullivan County?"

"Oh, when I was nothing but a dirty little, misbehaving bastard?" he said, with a chuckle.

"Yes."

Episode Twenty-Nine

WEEKS WENT BY WITH Laura and Craig living together platonically. As bruises faded and stitches were removed, love settled in her heart. C. W. returned to work after the New Year. Since he was only one flight down, he'd join her for lunch every day and left the office promptly at five, each night so they could dine together.

Except for a passionate kiss fueled by champagne on New Year's Eve, Craig had only placed kisses on her forehead or cheek. She had been skittish, at first. He'd tread lightly.

"When you're ready to take things to the next level, let me know," he said over dinner, with a mischievous gleam in his eyes. His look made her shiver.

Could she continue to stay in C.W. Banley's house, living like his sister, or should she return home? Should they become lovers? He'd left it up to her. She pondered her choices, feeling more blessed than ever.

By the fifteenth of January, she found herself free from painkillers and wanting exercise. Craig took her for gradually longer walks in Central Park. The touch of his hand on hers, a hug, his lips on her cheek, sparked a fierce desire in her for more.

That evening, they retired, to their separate rooms at ten thirty. Laura showered, then slipped, naked, into her silky robe. Her pulse kicked up and nerves started. A slight tremble sped through her. Was it fear or passion? Maybe both. She padded barefoot to the end of the hall.

Taking a deep breath, she raised a slightly shaky fist and knocked.

"Come in."

With a damp palm, she twisted the doorknob. He stood in nothing but boxers by the end of the huge bed. Her gaze sauntered over him, taking in every sexy inch. His body was almost perfect. Broad shoulders, a muscled chest with a smattering of brown hair, and a trim waist led to powerful thighs. Her mouth went dry and her pulse pounded in her ears. He crossed the room quickly.

"Does this mean what I think it does?"

"Yes. If you'll have me."

"Darling," he muttered into her hair, taking her into his arms as he nudged the door shut.

THE END

IF YOU ENJOYED THIS story, you might like others by Jean Joachim

BOTTOM OF THE NINTH
DAN ALEXANDER, PITCHER
MATT JACKSON, CATCHER
JAKE LAWRENCE, THIRD BASEMAN
NAT OWEN, FIRST BASE
BOBBY HERNANDEZ, SECOND BASE
SKIP QUINCY, SHORT STOP

FIRST & TEN SERIES
GRIFF MONTGOMERY, QUARTERBACK
BUDDY CARRUTHERS, WIDE RECEIVER
PETE SEBASTIAN, COACH
DEVON DRAKE, CORNERBACK
SLY "BULLHORN" BRODSKY, OFFENSIVE LINE
AL "TRUNK" MAHONEY, DEFENSIVE LINE
HARLEY BRENNAN, RUNNING BACK
OVERTIME, THE FINAL TOUCHDOWN
A KING'S CHRISTMAS
THE MANHATTAN DINNER CLUB
RESCUE MY HEART
SEDUCING HIS HEART
SHINE YOUR LOVE ON ME
TO LOVE OR NOT TO LOVE

HOLLYWOOD HEARTS SERIES
IF I LOVED YOU
RED CARPET ROMANCE

MEMORIES OF LOVE
MOVIE LOVERS
LOVE'S LAST CHANCE
LOVERS & LIARS
His Leading Lady (Series Starter)

NOW AND FOREVER SERIES
NOW AND FOREVER 1, A LOVE STORY
NOW AND FOREVER 2, THE BOOK OF DANNY
NOW AND FOREVER 3, BLIND LOVE
NOW AND FOREVER 4, THE RENOVATED HEART
NOW AND FOREVER 5, LOVE'S JOURNEY
NOW AND FOREVER, CALLIE'S STORY (prequel)

MOONLIGHT SERIES
SUNNY DAYS, MOONLIT NIGHTS
APRIL'S KISS IN THE MOONLIGHT
UNDER THE MIDNIGHT MOON
MOONLIGHT & ROSES (prequel)
LOST & FOUND SERIES
LOVE, LOST AND FOUND
DANGEROUS LOVE, LOST AND FOUND

NEW YORK NIGHTS NOVELS
THE MARRIAGE LIST
THE LOVE LIST
THE DATING LIST
SHORT STORIES
SWEET LOVE REMEMBERED

TUFFER'S CHRISTMAS WISH
THE SECOND PLACE HEART (Coming)

About the Author

JEAN JOACHIM IS A BEST-selling romance fiction author, with books hitting the Amazon Top 100 list since 2012. She writes contemporary romance, which includes sports romance and romantic suspense.

Dangerous Love Lost & Found, First Place winner in the 2015 Oklahoma Romance Writers of America, International Digital Award contest. *The Renovated Heart* won Best Novel of the Year from Love Romances Café. *Lovers & Liars* was a Rom-Con finalist in 2013. And *The Marriage List* tied for third place as Best Contemporary Romance from the Gulf Coast RWA.

To Love or Not to Love tied for second place in the 2014 New England Chapter of Romance Writers of America Reader's Choice contest.

She was chosen Author of the Year in 2012 by the New York City chapter of RWA. Married and the mother of two sons, Jean lives in New York City. Early in the morning, you'll find her at her computer, writing, with a cup of tea, and a secret stash of black licorice. Jean has 30+ books, novellas and short stories published. Find them here: http://www.jeanjoachimbooks.com

Sign up for her newsletter, on her website, or Facebook page, and be eligible for her private paperback sales.

https://www.facebook.com/pages/JeanJoachimAuthor/221092234568929?sk=app_100265896690345

Made in the USA
Columbia, SC
22 December 2017